Can You See Me?

Written by
Stephen Rickard

Many animals try to hide.

They do not want other animals to see them.

Some animals hide to stay safe.

Some animals hide to hunt for food.

What is the best way to hide?

Tawny frogmouth

These birds can look like part of a tree. This is called camouflage.

The birds often sit on a broken part of the tree. They look like the tree bark.

When they keep still, they are hard to see. They can stay safe.

Leopard

The leopard has spots all over its body. This camouflage makes it hard to be seen in the places where it lives.

The leopard hides to catch its prey. It creeps up on a deer or a zebra and then runs after it.

The leopard can run very fast.

Peacock flounder

This fish lives on the sea bed.
Its camouflage makes it hard
to see.

This helps it stay safe and catch
food.

This fish can change its colour.
This helps it stay hidden in different
places.

Jumping spider

The jumping spider is hard to see.

It hides so that it can catch its prey.

This spider is catching an ant.
The ant did not see the spider
until it was too late.

Flower mantis

The flower mantis is an insect that looks just like a flower.

It sits on a plant where it cannot be seen.

Other insects come to the plant to feed. The flower mantis can catch the insects and eat them.

You can see me!

Some animals have very bright colours. They are easy to see.

These animals are not good to eat. They have poison in them.

The bright colours say, "Do not eat me!".

Index

bright colours   14, 15

flower mantis   12, 13

jumping spider   10, 11

leopard   6, 7

peacock flounder   8, 9

tawny frogmouth   4, 5